DEDICATION

This book is dedicated to the joy, wonder and excitement the Christmas tradition brings to children and their families everywhere...

and to our niece Sydni, whos laughter rings out through the pages of this book, a very special girl who remains in my thoughts and heart daily.

The Christmas Dinosaur

by
By Angela and John Brix-Maffei

AuthorHouse™
1663 Liberty Drive, Suite 200
Bloomington, IN 47403
www.authorhouse.com
Phone: 1-800-839-8640

First published by AuthorHouse 10/20/2008

ISBN: 978-1-4389-0499-3 (sc)

Printed in the United States of America
Bloomington, Indiana

This book is printed on acid-free paper.

authorHOUSE®

Once upon a time, but not too long ago, in a very cold, magical, wintry place, a new Christmas tradition was born.

Among the snowy hills and big white fluffy mountains was a small, warm place that was home to many. Some say you can find this mystical place at the North Pole, although its exact location is unknown.

The Christmas Village is a very merry, yummy place where penguins, reindeer, and elves play.

What makes this magical place so merry and yummy is that the entire village is made of gingerbread and Christmas treats, which can sometimes cause a problem when there is much work to do.

Like today, Mr. Claus—better known as Santa Claus—was trying to round up his elves, as the Christmas toy factory needed to get busy.

Penny the penguin, however, had other ideas.

She gathered a few of the elves and took them outside for a pre-Christmas snowball fight.

While searching through the snow, Penny found an odd-looking snowball.

It was large, round, hard, and colored with green and purple spots.

Penny called the other elves over. This was not a snowball, after all, they thought. It looked like an egg.

They decided to dig up the egg, but what they did not realize was this was not an ordinary egg, and it was much, much bigger than they imagined.

The egg was so big that they could not lift it or even roll it back to the Christmas Village.

So after scratching their heads for a bit, they decided to go get Santa's sleigh and some of his reindeer.

Penny, the elves, and the reindeer loaded the egg into the sleigh and brought it home to Santa's house.

"PHEWF!" Penny sighed after they arrived ...

"PHEWF is right!" Rudolph the reindeer said. "That egg was heavy!"

Santa Claus was having a much-needed afternoon nap when he heard his sleigh pull in. He got dressed and walked outside. "What is that in my sled?" he asked Penny.

But just before she could answer Santa ... CRACK!

"Oh my! Ho ho!" Santa exclaimed.

CRACK ...

CRRRRAAAAACK!

All of a sudden, two large eyeballs popped out of the top of the egg, then two big nostrils, and then two tiny arms.

"Ho ho, a dinosaur!" Santa yelled.

Penny fainted.

The little dinosaur started to make all kinds of weird sounds. Then Santa walked over and put a red Santa hat on top of the baby dino's head.

Immediately, the baby dinosaur was quiet.

"What should we call him?" Santa asked.

"How about the Christmas Dinosaur?" said one of the elves.

Penny awoke when all the elves began to cheer. She shook her head, looked up at Santa, and said, "Have there ever been any dinosaurs at the North Pole before? I thought they were ex-stinky?"

"Ho ho!" Santa laughed. "You mean *extinct, and no, Penny, we have never had any dinosaurs here before, so that makes him very special.*

"I bet he is hungry. Penny, why don't you go tell Mrs. Claus what has happened and ask her for the biggest bottle of milk she can find."

With that, Penny ran off, returning moments later with a group of other penguins carrying a big bottle.

They began to feed the Christmas Dinosaur, and he ate and ate and ate.

He began to grow and grow and grow.

After many hours of feeding him, Penny and her friends decided to tuck him into bed in his very own gingerbread cabin and go get some sleep. A few hours later, the Christmas Dinosaur awoke.

"I hungry," he said. Looking around, he saw his blankie. It was made of cotton candy.

"Mmmmmm," he mumbled and took one big bite. He took another, then another, and soon his blankie was at the bottom of his tummy!

"I hungry," he said again. Looking down, he saw his bed. It was made of gingerbread.

"Mmmmmmmm," he grumbled and took one big bite. He took another, then another, and soon his entire bed was gone!

"I hungry more," he said. Walking around his cabin, he sniffed until he reached his door.

That too was made of gingerbread. "Mmmmmmmm," he said, and took one big bite. He took another, then another, and soon he was standing outside with only some small door crumbs at his feet!

Outside, everything was quiet. Everyone was still all snuggled in their beds. The Christmas Dinosaur looked around, and began to walk toward the toy factory.

Along the way, he found a beautifully decorated Christmas tree.

SNIFF … SNIFF. "Mmmmmmm." And with that, he quickly chomped down on one of the tree branches.

One by one, the Christmas Dinosaur pulled ornaments off the tree—ribbon, gold balls, candy canes, popcorn, and he even ate all the Christmas light bulbs off the tree.

"I hungry more, more, more!" he said, and then made his way down to Santa's toy factory.

Inside, he became an eating machine.

First he ate all the stuffing for the teddy bears.

Next he ate bouncy balls, soccer balls, basketballs, hockey pucks, hockey sticks, drum sets, coloring books, crayons, and even the wooden workbenches the elves used to sit on.

"I hungry more, more, more," he said. The Christmas Dinosaur then wandered back outside. Still, no one was to be found.

He began to walk, then all of a sudden, he stopped.

SNIFF … SNIFF … SNIFFF … MMMMMMM … SNIFF SNIFF.

The Christmas Dinosaur smelled his way across the village to Mrs. Claus's bakery.

Inside he went.

He saw cupcakes, tarts, pies, Christmas cake, chocolate, fudge, brownies, marshmallow goodies, gumdrops, gingerbread cookies, licorice, jars of colorful sprinkles.

Even peanut butter muffins covered the countertops.

Tray after tray, he ate all the baked goodies, until there was nothing left.

Christmas-colored red and green candy sprinkles went flying everywhere!

He even ate one or two of Mrs. Claus's baking pans!

Seconds later, the Christmas Dinosaur's mouth opened again, and...

BURP!!!!!!!!!!!

His burp was so loud, it woke everyone who was sleeping in the Christmas Village.

Mrs. Claus sat straight up in bed.

"THE BAKERY!" she yelled.

Penny, the penguins, the reindeer, and even Mr. and Mrs. Claus ran to the bakery.

There they found the Christmas Dinosaur lying on the floor with the biggest belly they had ever seen.

"Me no hungry anymore," said the Christmas Dinosaur.

"This is no good," said Mrs. Claus. "We must figure out what to do about his eating, or he will eat this entire village."

Just then, Penny laughed out loud and said, "His belly is bigger than Santa's is when he comes home after delivering the kids their presents on Christmas Eve and he eats all their cookies."

"That's it!" Mrs. Claus exclaimed. "We can send the Christmas Dinosaur with Santa on Christmas Eve, and he can help eat all the cookies and milk the kids leave behind."

"That's a great idea, Mrs. Claus," Santa said. "But only on two special conditions: We could use his size to help load the sled with all the Christmas presents, and you, Mrs. Claus, have to bake me more cookies to eat when I get back."

"You have a deal," Mrs. Claus said as she giggled.

"But one more thing," Penny said. "You're going to need a bigger sleigh and more reindeer to pull the two of you."

"We'll get right on it!" cheered the elves.

So over the next few days, the elves re-made all the Christmas toys that were eaten, and Mrs. Claus cleaned up the messy bakery.

The Christmas Dinosaur happily helped load the sleigh, eating snowballs in between lifting the red sacks of presents into Santa's sleigh.

Santa's elves worked very long into the night after having to build an extra sleigh for the Christmas Dinosaur to ride on.

Penny also had to round up more reindeer, and Mrs. Claus had to pack extra snacks for the trip.

Off into the night soared Santa with his hungry helper, the Christmas Dinosaur.

Of course, Mrs. Claus was nowhere to be seen, as she was busy baking again in preparation for the Christmas Village's Christmas Day celebration.

The Christmas Dinosaur happily rode around with Santa on Christmas Eve, and even more happily helped Santa eat all the cookies and drink all the milk the children left behind.

So kids, in light of this new Christmas tradition, you might want to leave just a few extra cookies out this Christmas.

After all, he is a very, very hungry dinosaur, but he loves Christmas just like the rest of us.

THE END !

Photo of the authors by Justin Murphy

About the Authors

This is Angela Brix-Maffei's first book but she is presently in the process of writing a novel that deals with her battle an antibiotic resistant 'super bug". After being admitted into a hospital for a routine day surgery she contracted a super bug. Her battle with this infection, the onlasting aftermath and the never ending pitfalls of the Canadian Health Care system are all documented in detail as she makes her way to recovery. Follow Angela as she learns about herself, humility and personal strength. Keep your eyes open for her second book, "Watching Leaves Fall." Coming soon.

John Brix-Maffei has written and published a novel called "The Wolf and the Sheepdog." This book describes the calls that the author has taken during his first five years of police work. Follow the author through a set of graphic and detailed short stories as you fill his work boots. get an insight to the policing world that you will never read about on any recruiting poster.

LaVergne, TN USA
07 October 2009
160128LV00005B